What Does Beauty Look Like?

What Does **Beauty** Look Like?

Written by
Monica G. Wood

Published by
Monica G. Wood
Hiz Temple, LLC
13016 Eastfield Road, Suite 200-219
Huntersville, North Carolina 28078

ISBN 978-0-692-83089-5

Cover Design by Hiz Temple, LLC
Layout by Rhue Still, Inc.

Printed in the United States of America

This book is dedicated to my dear niece, Ella Ruth.
May she always remember that as a child of God,
her beauty is not defined by others, but her beauty is defined by
what she sees in the mirror.
Love you to the moon and beyond,
Auntie Mo Mo

One day, Ella walked up to her mother and asked the question...

"Mommy, what does beauty look like?"

First, puzzled by the question, Ella's mother smiled and said,

"Baby, look out the window... beauty looks like leaves that drop from the trees on a cool fall afternoon."

Ella looked out the window at the falling leaves and smiled. Then, Ella asked again...

"Mommy, I see them, but what does beauty look like?"

Still puzzled, Ella's mother thought and thought. Then she said,

"Ella, beauty looks like the sun setting in the evening."

She looked out the window and pointed to the sun that was going down."

Ella looked out the window, saw the sun going down and smiled. Still not satisfied, she asked again...

"Mommy, what does beauty look like?"

Amazed that Ella kept asking the same question, her mother thought again about the question. Then replied...

"Ella, beauty looks like snow falling on a cold winter day."

Ella smiled as she remembered how much fun she had playing in the snow. But, still, Ella asked the question...

"Mommy, what does beauty look like?"

With a sparkle in her eyes and a big smile on her face, Ella's mother reached for her mirror. Handing it to her, she said,

"Look in the mirror, Ella. This is what beauty looks like...

...YOU!"

About The Author

Monica G. Wood, veteran communications and crisis management expert, is founder of **Hiz Temple, LLC**. Through the development of wearable items, workshops and inspiring messages, **Hiz Temple** encourages spiritual enrichment, self-respect and expressions of a bold love for God. Hiz Temple is not just a statement or a brand, it is a declaration and affirmation that we belong to God.

What Does Beauty Look Like?, is the first in a series of books created to help young girls and boys see value, good and beauty in all things.

Made in the USA
Middletown, DE
13 April 2017